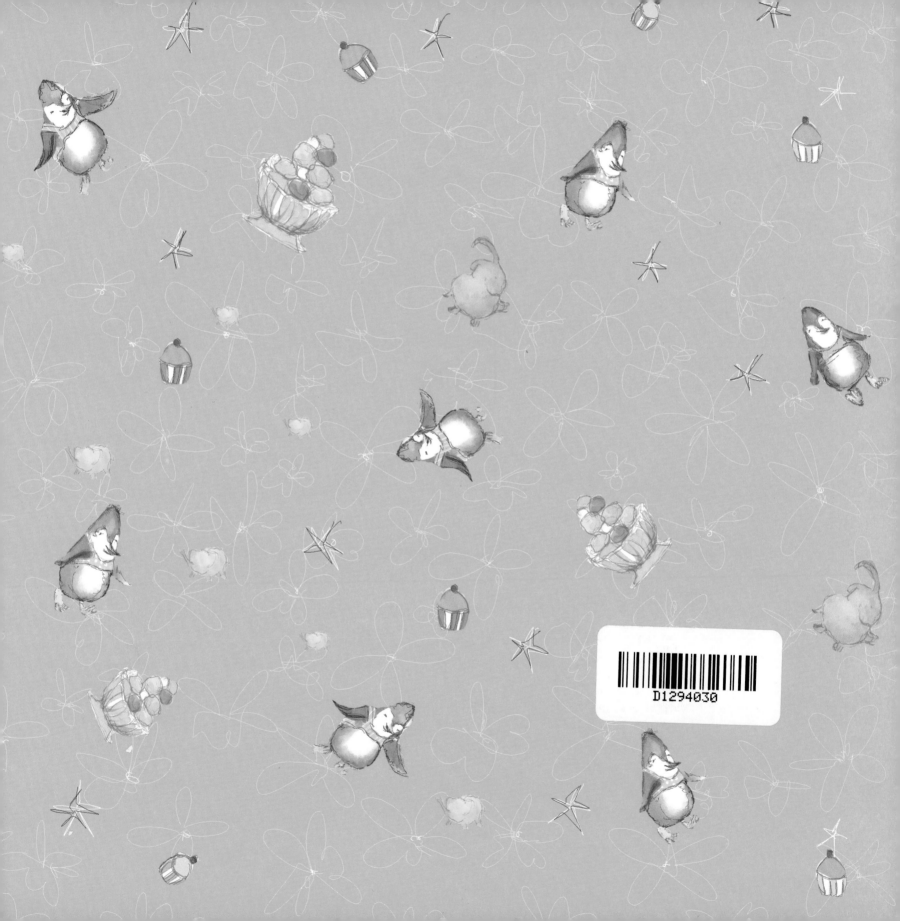

What if...?

LYNN JENKINS AND KIRRILI LONERGAN

Issy had a very busy mind.

She was always wondering
'What if ...' and often scaring
herself with what she imagined!

'What if there is a
monster in my cupboard?'

'What if an alien takes me
in the middle of the night?'

'What if a tree branch breaks my window and a vampire bat comes in?'

'What if my floor turns into
quicksand and swallows my bed?
With me in it!'

Mama listened to Issy. She held her hand, smiled and said,
'What if — two powerful little words.'

She lay down beside Issy. 'Let me have a turn.'

'What if clouds in the sky were purple and orange and green?'

'What if clouds smelled like fairy floss and popcorn?'

'What if trees had cupcakes
hanging from their
branches instead of leaves?'

'What if you could walk around on your hands all day?
How different would things look?'

'What if your hair grew purple and green spots?'

'What if your ears were upside down?
Would you hear differently?'

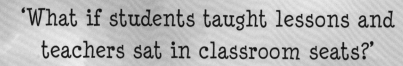

'What if students taught lessons and
teachers sat in classroom seats?'

'What if falibbertyschnozzel was a word?
What would it mean?'

'What if stars in the night sky were shaped like elephants?'

'What if penguins could be pets?'

'What if people walked around with undies on their heads?'

'What if the sun said good morning
every morning, and the moon said
good night every night?'

Issy laughed. 'That's all very silly, Mama!'

Mama laughed too and said, 'There are many possibilities after those two words "what" and "if". We can choose which direction they take us. Like, what if you chose the ending to this story? What would you choose if you could choose?'

Issy thought. 'I would choose …'

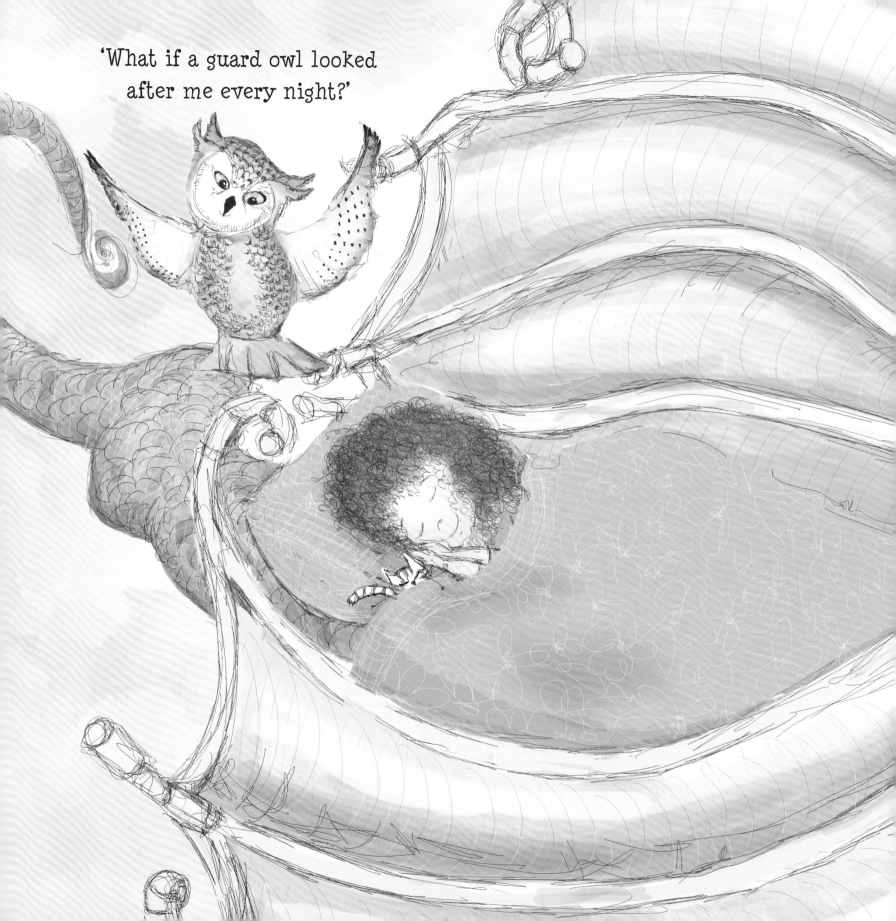

'What if a guard owl looked
after me every night?'

'What if my bed was secretly
a fire-breathing dragon with
glowing eyes?'

'What if stars came down from the sky and made
a path that led anywhere I wanted to go?'

'Like ...' Issy yawned,
'... a place where hot air
balloons took us everywhere.'

'Or, a place where eating ice cream is healthier than vegetables.'

Issy smiled as her eyes started to flutter shut.

'Or ...' Issy was asleep.

Mama smiled and brushed Issy's hair from her forehead with her hand. "'What" and "if" — two powerful little words that can take us magical places ...

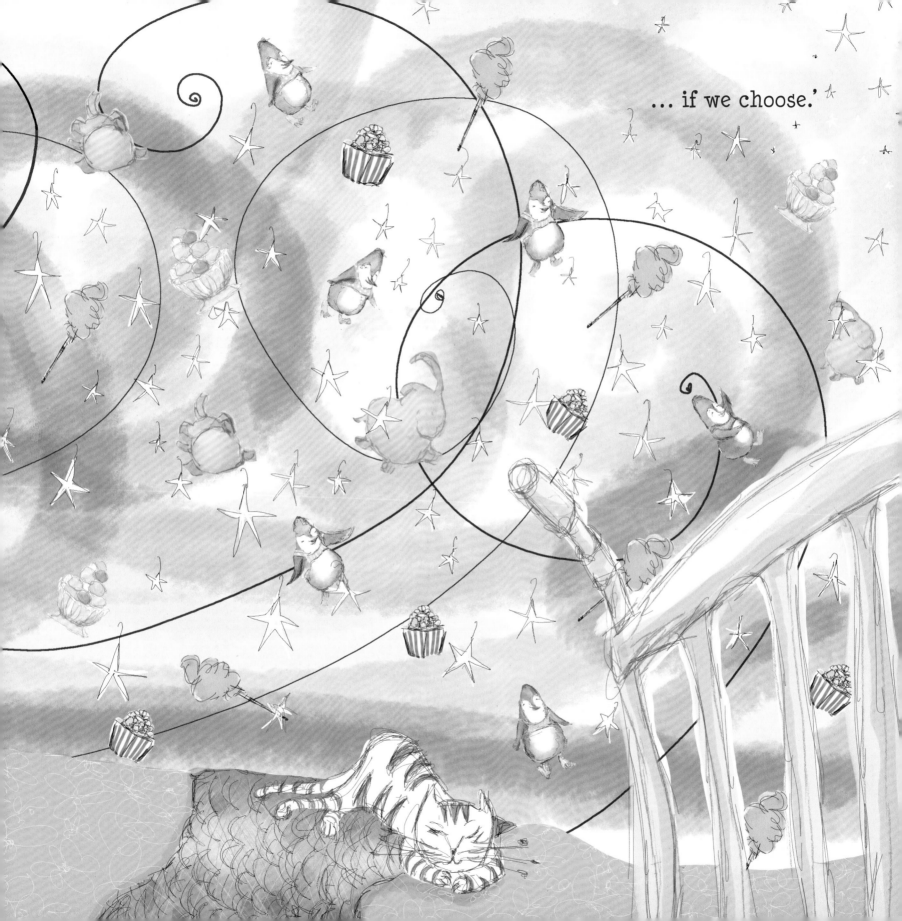

... if we choose.'

As always, to my little 'what if ... ers'. May you always
find the fun, playfulness and laughter in life. xx
– L.J.

For my Issy, this book celebrates all the fun,
wonder and what ifs that we share.
– K.L.

First published 2021

EK Books
an imprint of Exisle Publishing Pty Ltd
PO Box 864, Chatswood, NSW 2057, Australia
226 High Street, Dunedin, 9016, New Zealand
www.ekbooks.org

A CiP record for this book is available from the National Library of Australia.

ISBN 978-1-925820-97-3

Designed by Mark Thacker
Typeset in Minya Nouvelle 16 on 23pt
Printed in China

This book uses paper sourced under ISO 14001 guidelines from well-managed forests and other controlled sources.

2 4 6 8 10 9 7 5 3 1

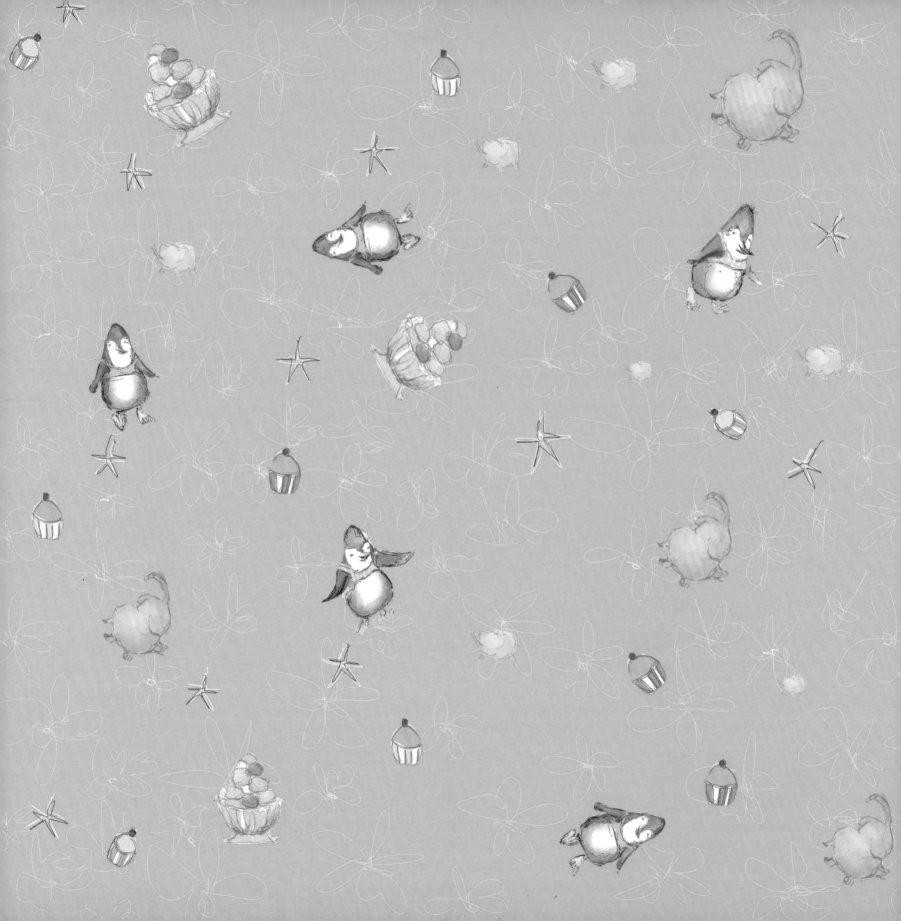